This book is dedicated to all of the children (and children at heart) in and around Beverly, Massachusetts.

Cheers to you for helping keep the magic and joy of Shoebert's visit to our coastline alive and well.

I hope you enjoy this story and all of the memories of Shoebert for years to come !

A Newburyport native, Sarah MacBurnie (Liporto), a.k.a. Sarah Hazel, moved to the Beverly, MA area in 1998. Sarah always wrote as a child and continued to do so until College when life got busy.

Her writer's block was freed up in 2022 when she wrote her first Children's Book Shoebert: A Very Brave Seal and The Impossible Journey Paperback —and published it on her daughter's 11th birthday, December 9, 2022.

In addition to writing children's books Sarah is a Mom, wife, and real estate professional who also works in reiki and yoga. Sarah prides herself on being open to what the Universe has in store for her.

"I miss all of the people I used to see."
Shoebert thought to himself as he
swam around inside an aquarium tank.

"Now we will be able to keep track of you,"
the aquarium vet said.

Shoebert was in an aquarium far from his home. In fact, it was MILES away.

"You are healthy enough to go back into the ocean," the aquarium worker said to Shoebert.

Shoebert tried to decide which way
he should go.

www.loremipsum.com

LOCAL NEWS

BREAKING NEWS: Scientists confirm that Shoebert the famous seal has made his way back home. All the way from the Aquarium miles away !!!

Seals have a keen sense and can use their whiskers to guide them, even when they are really far away from their home.

"Even though this is not quite where I wanted to be, I am happy to be back." Shoebert said.

The town's people were overjoyed to know that Shoebert was somewhere near the shore.

Shoebert was happy to know he was close by the town where people made him feel so loved.

And the town really loves Shoebert and cannot wait to hear what he does next!

But until then, the children sleep well at night knowing that Shoebert is close by.

The
End

Made in United States
North Haven, CT
24 January 2023

31528092R00015